Maybelle

Goes to School

Read all about Maybelle's
other adventures!

Maybelle

Goes to School

Katie Speck

illustrations by

Paul Rátz de Tagyos

Henry Holt and Company ℗ New York

For my sister Brenda,
Maybelle's long and loyal friend —K. S.

Henry Holt and Company, LLC
Publishers since 1866
175 Fifth Avenue, New York, New York 10010
mackids.com

Library of Congress Cataloging-in-Publication Data
Speck, Katie, author.
Maybelle goes to school / Katie Speck ; illustrations by Paul Rátz de Tagyos. — First edition.
pages   cm
Summary: When Mrs. Peabody makes her Ten-Layer Tower of Taste for the school bake sale,
Maybelle the cockroach cannot resist sampling the cake, but when she wakes up to find herself
on the way to the lunchroom she knows she is in big trouble—especially after she
discovers she has to rescue her friend, Henry the flea.
ISBN 978-0-8050-9158-8 (hardcover) — ISBN 978-1-62779-419-0 (e-book)
1. Cockroaches—Juvenile fiction. 2. Fleas—Juvenile fiction. 3. Insects—Juvenile fiction.
4. Cake—Juvenile fiction. 5. Schools—Juvenile fiction. [1. Cockroaches—Fiction. 2. Fleas—Fiction.
3. Insects—Fiction. 4. Cake—Fiction. 5. Schools—Fiction.]
I. Rátz de Tagyos, Paul, illustrator. II. Title.
PZ7.S741185Maf 2015   [Fic]—dc23   2014034625

First edition—2015
Printed in the United States of America by Worzalla,
Stevens Point, Wisconsin

3   5   7   9   10   8   6   4   2

Contents

❂ 1 ❂

The Tower of Taste

Maybelle the Cockroach was obeying all The Rules: *When it's light, stay out of sight; if you're spied, better hide; never meet with human feet.* She hadn't had an adventure in some time. That suited her fine. She wasn't fond of adventures.

She was fond of cake.

One evening, Maybelle watched from her home under the refrigerator while

1

Myrtle Peabody baked and frosted her famous Ten-Layer Tower of Taste. Mrs. Peabody was quite sure there were ABSOLUTELY, POSITIVELY NO BUGS at Number 10 Grand Street. She left the cake uncovered on the kitchen counter.

Maybelle thought Mrs. Peabody's cake was the most beautiful thing she had ever seen. She intended to have a bite. Or two.

"Don't worry," she said to her friend Henry the Flea. Henry lived and dined on Ramona, the Peabodys' cat. "It's dark.

No one will see me and call the Bug Man. And I won't be squashed, either; the Peabodys' feet will be in bed."

"Keep your eyes open, kiddo," Henry said. "It's easy to fall asleep when you eat too much. You could wake up on that cake and find yourself in Trouble." Henry would know. He once went to sleep on a poodle after a tasty meal. He almost got a flea dip.

"I won't fall asleep," Maybelle said. "There's a different fruit jam between every layer of that cake. I'm going to sample them all and be home before morning."

Henry looked at the Tower of Taste. "What's the special occasion, I wonder?"

Maybelle should have wondered, too. When a cake rises to ten layers, Something is up.

⊙ 2 ⊙

The Light Dawns

Z Z Z Z

After everyone was asleep, Maybelle scuttled out into the dark kitchen and up onto the counter.

Mrs. Peabody's cake rose high in the air. Maybelle began at the bottom and tasted her way up. She sampled pink icing and sugar flowers.

And she did exactly

what Henry had warned her not to do: she ate too much and fell asleep. By morning she snored softly in the blueberry jam between the fourth and fifth layers of the Tower of Taste.

Meanwhile, as the sun came up, the Peabodys began bustling around the house.

While Henry hid on Ramona's belly, Mr. Peabody brushed the cat's black stripes. "Ramona must surely be the prettiest, shiniest tabby cat anywhere," he said. He tied a red bow around her neck JUST SO to make it official. She did not look pleased.

Mrs. Peabody set

her cake on a platter and arranged candied fruit on top in a little pile, JUST SO.

"My cake will be the grandest one at the elementary school bake sale this year," she said to Mr. Peabody. Mrs. Peabody never passed up a chance to show off. "The Tower of Taste will put Mildred Snodgrass's cake to shame."

"ABSOLUTELY, POSITIVELY!" the Peabodys said together.

Right then, Maybelle woke up where she had no business being and knew she was in Trouble.

꩜ 3 ꩜

On the Road

At the same moment, the doorbell rang. *Ding-dong!* It was Samuel and Samantha, the Snerdly twins from next door.

"Can I borrow a flea?" Samuel asked.

"He's starting a flea circus," Samantha said. "All he has so far is a pair of pants."

Samuel opened his hand. The Peabodys leaned down to see what looked like a tiny ball of thread.

"Very nice, dear," Mrs. Peabody said. "But you cannot borrow a flea from this house. There are Absolutely, Positively NO BUGS at Number 10 Grand Street."

"May I please borrow Ramona?" Samantha said. "My hamster went under the clothes dryer."

"It's her turn to show Something Interesting at lunch today," Samuel said.

"Why, certainly not!" Mr. Peabody said. "Ramona could not stand the excitement of going to school."

"On the other hand, dear Herbert,

she looks so pretty. It would be a shame if no one but us admired her."

Mr. Peabody had to agree. "We'll bring her over to school when we bring the cake for the bake sale," Mr. Peabody said.

So the Peabodys put the cake and the cat on the back seat of their car.

Mr. Peabody started the engine, *VROOOM!* And off they went.

Maybelle's heart pounded. She peeked out of the cake through the tiny hole in the icing where she'd crawled in. "*Psst!* Henry, where are we going?"

Henry parted Ramona's fur. He didn't remind Maybelle that he'd warned her not to fall asleep in her food. "I don't

know," he said. "But maybe there will be a Golden Retriever there for me to bite. I never give up hope, kiddo. As for you, you'd better stay out of sight. Wherever we're going, cockroaches aren't welcome."

And that was something Maybelle already knew.

4

Nobody Home

When Maybelle peeked out of the cake again, what she saw through her hole in the icing made her want to go straight home. She was on the bake sale table in the lunchroom of Interesting Times Elementary School. The Peabodys and other large humans stood close by.

Across the room the Lunch Lady marched up and down the cafeteria line, clattering pots and pans. *Bang! Clang!* She wore a hairnet and big, squeaky shoes. *Squeak, squeak! Bang! Clang!* It was all very alarming.

Henry had told Maybelle to stay hidden. But she needed to ask him how to get home again. That meant she had to find Ramona. And to find Ramona, she had to see above the crowd.

She slipped out of the safe, dark, blueberry jam. She scurried up, up, up the side of the Tower of Taste as fast as she could. She dove into the candied fruit Mrs. Peabody had arranged on top JUST SO.

Then she looked around from behind a cherry.

Maybelle saw Ramona in her carrying case on a chair nearby. She was staring at Maybelle. She did not look friendly.

"Henry! Are you there?" Maybelle called. "I want to go home!"

Ramona laid her ears back. "*Hisssss!*" she said.

Not a sound from Henry.

Maybelle's heart sank. Henry wasn't on his cat.

He must have moved on to something Golden and Delicious.

☺ 5 ☺

A Friend Flies By

"BZZZRRRT! Coming down! Coming down!" A very large housefly landed next to Maybelle. He rubbed his legs together. "ZZZZRT!"

The fly looked familiar. He had bug eyes and hairy legs. His feet smelled.

"Maurice?"

"Hey there, Missy! BRRZZZT! Got yourself a nice cake there."

Maybelle had seldom been happier to see a friend. She didn't even mind that Maurice was noisy and irritating. "I don't want this cake. I want to go home. I want to find Henry. Have you seen any Golden Retrievers?"

"Nope. I'm waiting for lunch. Today is Mystery Meat." Maurice rubbed his legs

together faster and faster. "Catch you later, Missy! Going up! Going up! BRZZZRT!" He was gone again.

Maurice wasn't likely to be much help. Maybelle would have to find Henry by herself.

While the Peabodys waited for Samantha Snerdly to present Ramona to the Lower School, Mildred Snodgrass placed her cake next to Mrs. Peabody's Ten-Layer Tower of Taste.

"Look, Herbert! My cake is taller and prettier than Mildred's Mocha Majesty," Mrs. Peabody said.

"And Ramona has the finest and shiniest coat any tabby cat could have."

"ZRRRT!" Maurice buzzed by, and Mr. Peabody flapped his hand in the air.

"ZRRRT! ZRRRT!"

"Shoo! Shoo!" Both Peabodys flapped their hands. "We must guard our cake, Herbert. This place has bugs!" Mrs. Peabody said.

Maybelle could not wait another minute to find Henry.

And so, with the Peabodys much too close for comfort, Maybelle had to sneak down from the top of the Tower of Taste in broad daylight. And scurry through humans, with eyes to see her and feet to squash her, and . . .

Oh dear! She was *never* going to eat cake again!

❦ 6 ❧

Eight Legs

Maybelle didn't know where she was going, but she intended to keep going there until she found Henry. With her heart pounding, she skittered out of the lunchroom, down a hall, and into the first room she came to.

"Eyes on your work please, children," the teacher said.

Small humans! Lots of them! Luckily

they paid no attention to Maybelle as she ducked into a row of cozy dark cubbyholes.

"Henry? Are you here?" she called softly. No answer.

Maybelle began to explore. In one cubby there was a little red race car sticking out of a backpack. In another was—*sniff*—a peanut butter and jelly sandwich in a brown paper bag. She was on her way to a third cubby when she noticed a terrarium on the shelf above her. A sign said ROSIE THE TARANTULA.

"My, my. Aren't you a lovely, plump thing," Rosie said. "Come a little closer and let me have a look at you." Rosie was very large and very hairy.

Maybelle crept nearer. "Have you seen a flea named Henry or a Golden Retriever?"

"Sorry, dearie. I can't hear you. You'll have to come closer."

Maybelle crawled to the side of the terrarium and spoke as loudly as she dared. "I need to find Henry. I want to go home," she said.

"What was that, darling?" Rosie said.

Rosie's eyes were black and beady. Maybelle didn't like the look of her. But she climbed to the top of Rosie's home, squeezed through the wire cover, and went right up to the spider's face. Rosie could surely hear her now.

"Have you seen a Golden Retriever?" Maybelle shouted up at her.

Rosie crouched ever so slightly on her eight legs. "Humm," she said. Or was it more like . . .

"YUM!"

Rosie sprang. Maybelle turned and fled back the way she had come as fast as her six legs could carry her.

Just then, the lunch bell rang. *Clang!* Maybelle dove into the brown bag she'd passed earlier and waited in the peanut butter and jelly to see what would happen next.

ʚ 7 ɞ

Henry Under Glass

In the lunchroom, Beau Snodgrass wound up his little red car and raced it down the table. Next to him, Samantha Snerdly set out her lunch. While Samantha blew her straw wrapper across the table, Maybelle poked her head out of Samantha's sandwich and wiped the peanut butter from her eyes. And there, right in front of her, was a stuffed golden dog. It was under the arm of the little human in the next chair. Could it be a Golden Retriever?

"Henry, are you there?" Maybelle said.

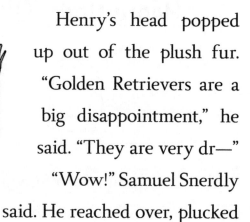

Henry's head popped up out of the plush fur. "Golden Retrievers are a big disappointment," he said. "They are very dr—"

"Wow!" Samuel Snerdly said. He reached over, plucked Henry from the dog's head, and then ran off.

"Oh no!" Maybelle said.

She couldn't go home without Henry. But what had happened to him?

She soon found out.

Samuel Snerdly came back holding a

plate with an upside-down drinking glass on it. A little sign scribbled on a napkin said FLEA CIRCUS: DRESSED FLEA.

Henry was under the glass. And he was wearing pants!

That was bad enough. But little humans were leaning over and *peering* at Henry. Maybelle almost fainted with the horror of it.

"Don't worry, Henry, I'll get help!"

Henry didn't hear her. He stood gazing down at his pants.

Maybelle wasn't big enough to knock the glass over and free Henry. But she knew someone who was. Someone with stripes.

Clang! Bang! Squeak, squeak!

"Children! Eat every bite of your food if you want to grow up big and strong," the Lunch Lady said.

It was then that Samantha noticed her sandwich had antennae. *Yuck!* She threw it under the table. She could grow up big and strong another day.

Maybelle struggled out of the sticky peanut butter and set off across the lunchroom. She had to get to Ramona. But she couldn't help noticing all the crumbs along the way. Lunchrooms were delightfully messy.

Of course, she shouldn't think about food with Henry in trouble.

On the other hand, she had to keep up her strength. She snatched a taste of this and a nibble of that as she scurried along beneath the lunch tables.

When she reached the cakes, she climbed up, up, up the Tower of Taste and waited. Maybelle had a plan.

8

Yoo-hoo!

"Boys and girls! Here is today's Something Interesting," said the Principal. "Go ahead, Samantha."

Samantha Snerdly took Ramona out of her carrying case. The Peabodys glowed. Ramona did not look pleased.

Maybelle stood tall atop the pile of fruit on Mrs. Peabody's cake.

"This is Ramona Peabody," Samantha said in a small voice.

Maybelle waved her antennae. Ramona's eyes widened.

"Hiss!" Ramona said.

Mrs. Peabody saw Maybelle at the same moment Ramona did. "Herbert! There's a cockroach on my cake!" she whispered.

Samantha went on. "She is a tabby cat. She has tiger stripes. See how shiny her stripes are?" Samantha held Ramona up high.

Maybelle wiggled her antennae and five of her six legs at the cat.

"Rrrrrr," Ramona said.

"It's standing up and waving its nasty little feet!" Mrs. Peabody said.

Samantha struggled to hold Ramona up even higher so everyone could see her. "She's really big, too."

From the top of the cake, Maybelle waved her antennae and four of her legs and jumped up and down.

"Oh no!" Mrs. Peabody wailed.

"RAAOO-
OOOW!"
Ramona yowled.
She scratched
Samantha, leaped
into the air, and
landed on Mrs. Peabody's
famous Tower of Taste. *SPLAT!*

But Maybelle was already off and running.

⚬ 9 ⚬

Ramona to the Rescue

"**M**y cake!" Mrs. Peabody screeched.

"Our cat!" Mr. Peabody roared. "Catch her!"

The Peabodys ran after Ramona. Ramona sprinted after Maybelle—"*Spit! Hiss!*"—and Maybelle fled across the lunchroom to Henry's glass.

Ramona chased Maybelle across the tables. The cat ran so fast, she slipped on a glob of Mystery Meat and skidded into some macaroni and cheese. But she didn't slow down. She leaped after Maybelle through a

pile of succotash and knocked over cartons of milk. Still, she didn't slow down.

Little humans squealed and giggled and jumped out of their chairs. Lunch trays crashed to the floor. Pudding cups exploded. The Lunch Lady shouted, "Order! Order!" But even *that* didn't slow Ramona down.

Maybelle had never run faster, but she could feel Ramona's whiskers close behind her.

Samuel Snerdly's Dressed Flea under a glass was just ahead.

Oh, poor Henry! Maybelle thought. She dashed up the table and onto the top of the glass. Ramona was so close and going so fast that she slid into it—and knocked it over!

꩜ 10 ꩜

Henry Wears the Pants

Henry was free.

"Come on, Henry! Let's go!" Maybelle said.

But Henry wasn't going anywhere in a hurry. His pants were too big. The best he could do was hold them up and shuffle along.

"Take the pants off, Henry!"

"No," Henry said. "I won't."

Maybelle couldn't flee without her friend, but she was in terrible danger. Ramona crouched over her.

Before Ramona could pounce, Mr. Peabody seized his cat. She was covered with Today's Lunch Menu.

"Ohhh," Mr. Peabody moaned. He held her at arm's length so she wouldn't ruin his clothes. "The beautiful stripes! The shiny coat! Gone!"

"Our poor Precious! It isn't her fault this school is

full of revolting bugs," Mrs. Peabody said. "I expect you to complain to the Principal, Herbert."

"I intend to, dear," Mr. Peabody said.

The Peabodys carried their cat off in a huff.

Maybelle grabbed Henry and hid under a table while the children in the lunchroom settled down.

"I'm keeping the pants, Maybelle," Henry announced. "They make my legs look longer."

Maybelle rolled her eyes. "Well, come on, then." She took one of Henry's legs and pulled him along. "We have to figure out a way to get home."

"We have to go the same way we came," Henry said.

"Then we can't let the Peabodys leave school without us." Maybelle pulled Henry faster. She headed back to the Tower of Taste.

All she had to do to get there was cross the lunchroom dragging a Dressed Flea. And scurry through dozens of small humans with little eyes to see her and little feet to squash her. And . . .

Oh dear!

☙ 11 ❧

ZOOOM!

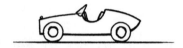

On the way to the Tower of Taste, Maybelle stopped to rest under a napkin.

"BRRZZZT! Coming down!" Maurice landed on the napkin and peeked at Maybelle and Henry.

"Whoa! I like your pants, little fella." He turned to Maybelle. "There's better stuff to eat around here than a napkin with mustard on it, Missy," he said to her.

"Try the Mystery Meat. Yum! BRZZZT!" Maurice rubbed his greasy legs together.

"I'm scared and tired, Maurice. I just want to go home. I've got to get back to the Tower of Taste."

"You need wheels," Maurice said. "There's a kid playing with a windup car at the next table. Follow me."

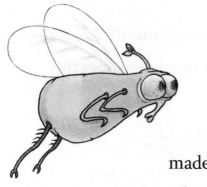

With Maurice flying overhead and buzzing directions, Maybelle and Henry made their dangerous way up onto the table.

"Now, Missy," Maurice called down, "hide behind a carton of milk. When the car goes by, jump in. ZRRRT!" Maurice did a loop-the-loop in the air. "BZRRRT!"

Beau Snodgrass wound up his little red race car as tight as tight could be. He let it go. *ZOOM!*

"Hang on to me, Henry." Maybelle counted *one, two, three.* As the car raced past, she jumped in.

WHOA! That little car was fast! It tore down the table, over the edge, and into the air.

"Going up!" Maurice yelled. "BZZRT!"

The two friends were flying! *ZOOM!*

๑ 12 ๑

The Last Straw

The car hit the floor with a *thump*. Maybelle and Henry almost bounced out. Then the tires squealed and the car took off across the lunchroom.

The Red Racer was fast, but—

"Steer!" Henry cried. They just missed hitting a tennis shoe.

"I don't know how, Henry!"

Maybelle and Henry squeezed their eyes closed.

Meanwhile, the Peabodys looked at what was left of Mrs. Peabody's famous Ten-Layer Tower of Taste. It was sadly reduced in height. There were paw prints all over it. There was a bit of cat hair stuck in the icing.

"Such a shame about your cake," Mildred Snodgrass said. "I myself don't keep cats." She gazed proudly at her own Mocha Majesty. Now *she* had the prettiest cake at the bake sale.

"It isn't Ramona's fault. This school is crawling with bugs," Mr. Peabody said.

Mrs. Peabody sniffed and wiped

her eyes. "This is Absolutely, Positively DREADFUL! If I see another bug, I'm going to—"

Just then, the little Red Racer rolled over her toes.

☙ 13 ☙

On the Road Again

Mrs. Peabody looked down. "EEEEEK!" she shrieked. "They're teaching bugs to *drive* at this school! I want to go home, Herbert!"

The Racer tipped over on the other side of Mrs. Peabody's shoe and spilled Henry and Maybelle onto the floor. Maybelle ran for cover with Henry still holding on to her.

"This place is full of bugs," Mr. Peabody complained to the Principal.

"I was too busy watching a Certain Cat destroy my lunchroom to notice any bugs," the Principal said.

"I'll have you know my wife was just attacked by a cockroach driving a car!"

The Principal smiled. "We all know that cockroaches don't drive cars, sir."

"It was a very *small* car." Mr. Peabody sniffed.

While the Peabodys complained, Maybelle hid in the mess that had been the Tower of Taste. She was going home the way she came. Henry joined her.

"I can't get out of here fast enough, Henry. This place is full of humans."

"BRZZZRT! Coming down!" Maurice landed on the platter. "Whoa, Missy. You were pretty hard on this cake."

"I don't want to talk about it," Maybelle said. "We're going home. Do you want to come?"

"Not a chance." Maurice rubbed his legs together. "ZRRRT! I'm hoping that food on the floor out there starts to rot.

Then, oh boy!" Maurice looked at Henry. "The pants make your legs look longer, kid. BRZZZZT! Going up!" He was gone.

Mr. and Mrs. Peabody put their cake and their cat on the back seat of the car. Mr. Peabody started the engine. *VROOM!* Off they went to Number 10 Grand Street, where there were ABSOLUTELY, POSITIVELY NO BUGS.

Myrtle Peabody was quite sure of it.

⚬ 14 ⚬

Better Luck Next Time

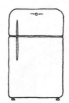

"Mildred Snodgrass will *not* have the best cake at the school bake sale again next year, Herbert."

Back home in her kitchen, Mrs. Peabody was already planning a new cake. She would call it her Seventeen-Layer Skyscraper Supreme.

"And Ramona will have a shiny coat again soon," Mr. Peabody said.

For now, Ramona was wrapped in a towel, still wet from a bath. She did not look pleased.

Ding-dong! The doorbell rang. The Snerdly twins were back.

"Thank you for letting me borrow Ramona," Samantha said. "Our Principal said she was the Most Interesting Thing that has ever happened in the lunchroom."

Mr. Peabody smiled proudly. "Why, of course she was."

"And he said she could never, ever come to school again."

The twins turned to go. "If you see a Dressed Flea," Samuel said over his shoulder, "would you mind getting the pants back?"

The Peabodys looked at each other. "*Whatever* is the child talking about? There are no bugs in this house. ABSOLUTELY, POSITIVELY!"

Under the refrigerator, Maybelle and Henry rested from their adventure.

"All in all, it was a good day," Henry said. "The Golden Retriever was dry. But

I may have gotten a bad one. I'll have to try again. I never give up hope."

"In the meantime, we've got to do something about those pants," Maybelle said.

"Everyone liked seeing me in my pants. I'm keeping them."

"Well then, I'll have to turn up the cuffs so you can jump. And I'll use one of Ramona's whiskers to make you a belt."

Henry could hop as high as ever when she was done. Maybelle had to admit he looked handsome, too.

That night she thought about Mrs. Peabody's Seventeen-Layer Skyscraper Supreme. Now *there* was something to look forward to! And she wouldn't fall asleep in it. Absolutely, Positively Not. She didn't want to end up at school again.

On the other hand, she wondered what it would be like to have a pair of pants. Or maybe a dress. Yes, a dress with pink polka dots to match the pink of her bow. And small humans waiting in line to see her. A sign would say DRESSED COCKROACH.

Such interesting possibilities!

Maybelle fell asleep in her own little bed, dreaming about cake and polka dots. The nice thing was, she would wake up in the very same place.